CON

THE GREATEST LOVE

THE NINE LIVES OF GABRIELLE: FOR THREE SHE STAYS - BOOK 3

LAURA MARIANI

the
PEOPLE
ALCHEMIST

ABOUT THE AUTHOR

Laura Mariani is an Author, Speaker and Entrepreneur.

She started her consulting business after a successful career as Senior HR Director within global brands in FMCG, Retail, Media and Pharma.

Laura is incredibly passionate about helping other women to break through barriers limiting their personal and/or professional fulfilment. Her best selling nonfiction *STOP IT! It is all in your head* and the *THINK, LOOK & ACT THE PART* series have been described as success and transformation 101.

She is a Fellow of the Chartered Institute of Personnel & Development (FCIPD), Fellow of the Australian Human Resources Institute (FAHRI), Fellow of the Institute of Leadership & Management (FInstLM), Member of the Society of Human Resources Management (SHRM) and Member of the Change Institute.

She is based in London, England with a strong penchant for travel and visiting new places. She is a food lover, ballet fanatic, passionate about music, art, theatre. She likes painting and drawing (for self-expression not selling but hey, you never know…), tennis, rugby, and of course fashion (the Pope is Catholic after all).

www.thepeoplealchemist.com
@PeopleAlchemist
instagram.com/lauramariani_author

NEW FICTION OUT ON 13 SEPTEMBER

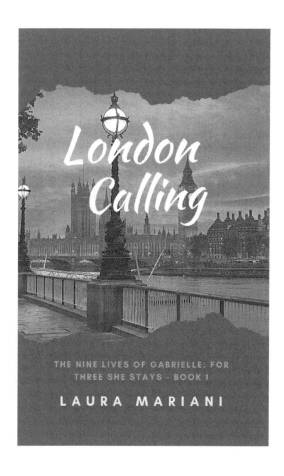

ALSO OUT 13 SEPTEMBER

NEW NON-FICTION BY LAURA MARIANI

ALSO BY LAURA MARIANI

Fiction

Gabrielle, from the diary of

The prequel to The Nine lives of Gabrielle:

For Three She Plays, For Three She Strays and last Three She Stays

As Gabrielle writes in her morning pages, she is flooder with vivid memories of the past and intense responses to the present …

She re-examines her choices throughout her life.

Can someone escape their self-identity?

For Three She Plays - Book 1 - 3

A New York Adventure

Troubled after the break-up of a long term relationship, Gabrielle sets out for a sabbatical in New York.

A travelogue searching for self, pleasure and fun. And the Big Apple doesn't disappoint.

Searching for Goren

Why are we always choosing people who don't allow intimacy? Is it because deep down we don't want it?

Tasting Freedom

As her trip to New York comes to an end, her shackles bare falling and Gabrielle begins to taste, finally, freedom.

For Three She Strays - Book 1 - 3

Paris Toujours Paris

They met in Paris. It was lust at first sight.

It wasn't easy for him to feel this way.

"Dear Gabrielle: Don't be afraid of how much I desire you," Le P.D.G. said to her in a note.

Me Myself and Us

Before meeting Le P.D.G., Gabrielle was a provincial middle-class girl who, against the odds, had made it in the oppressively male-dominated world.

He opened her up to sexual and emotional freedom she had never before experienced. But, despite his claims to her being the woman in his life, that did not imply she was the only one...

Freedom Over Me

Until meeting Le P.D.G, Gabrielle's experience of life was mainly secondhand, observed, and never viscerally involved.

Relationships aren't easy; they take a different take because of the memories and stories transformed during crucial moments.

Non-Fiction

STOP IT! It is all in your head

The RULE BOOK to Smash The infamous glass ceiling - For women & young women everywhere — personal transformation & success 101.

The Think, Look & Act The Part Series.

Think The Part

Upgrade your consciousness and mind-set. Make winning a key part of your life and business.

Look The Part

Upgrade your personal brand. Make presenting your unique Best Self a key part of your life and business.

Act The Part

A personal coach to act in spite of fear, right here, right now.

More non-fiction books and courses are coming soon.

For new releases, giveaways and pre-release specials check www.thepeoplealchemist.com

You can also buy my books and courses directly from Laura Mariani at www.payhip.com/LauraMariani

ThePeopleAlchemist Press publishes self help, inspirational and transformational books, resources and products to help #TheWomanAlchemist in every woman to change her life/ career and transmute any circumstance into gold, a bit like magic to **Unlock Ignite Transform.**

ISBN: 978-1-915501-22-6

THE GREATEST LOVE

I hope you all find what you are looking for

Your task is not to seek for LOVE,
but merely to seek and find all the barriers within yourself
that you have built against it

Rumi

"My darling, my love,

I can't be clever or aloof with you: I adore you too much for that.

You have no idea how detached I can be with people I don't hold dear. Or perhaps you do.

You have shattered my barriers. And I don't begrudge you for it.

There are not enough words to tell you what I feel,
It's a feeling I only get every time you're near, and I fear waking from this dream.

Back in your arms is where I want to be once again.
Nothing ever feels so right as when you hold me tight with your arms wrapped around me.

I nearly forgot what love was like until I met you.
Your first touch, first kiss, the first time you held me close.
And as time passed, I knew you'd be my last.
I love you more than I ever believed I was capable of.

You have seen a glimpse into a past long gone and forgotten —a past when I was still searching for myself.

You have shown me so much, more than you'll ever know. You have shown me the best of me, the higher me I had lost.

It is just impossible for me to say how truly grateful I am.

You make me feel like I can fly.

I don't think you comprehend what you do to me because it's impossible to see. I never told you what I feel when you hold my hand.

I've found my home in your arms, where I can finally learn to let go.

In your arms, I am at ease; the world disappears until it is only you and I, and nothing else matters.

In your arms, I am free; I can be more than I ever thought possible and be stronger.

You cleaned up the mess and healed my wounds, and now I'm beginning to be whole again.

In your arms, I've found my purpose, and there's nothing I can't do, no limits I can't transcend.
     In your arms, anything is possible.

In your arms, I find safety like no other, and I can breathe deep,
     knowing you'll always keep me close and never hurt me.

So please, my darling, hold me close, don't let me go.
     My heart belongs to you. This you must know.

I want to be here with you, not only for today but forever in your arms stay.

In your arms, I am home".

D ays had gone by since he had first read it. Mr Wonderful had kept Gabrielle's handwritten note neatly folded in his wallet, the only single reminder of the events. Life had continued unchanged since then.

He was, of course, happy: he could not envision a life without her. But Martin's comments were playing in his head nonstop.

"And whose fault is that?" Martin had said. "She is a flesh and blood woman with her faults and failures. Flesh and blood, my friend".

"Yes, she was", he had discovered in the letter from her ex-lover, "fresh and blood, sweat and tears. He had never seen 'That' Gabrielle", he thought.

"And you have put her on a pedestal, idolised her. You can't make passionate love to someone you are afraid to break; even I know that" Martin had noted.

He was right: Mr Wonderful was afraid to lose and break her; he had idolised her.

"You have shown me the best of me, the higher me I had lost". Gabrielle had written.

And she was *"truly grateful"* for it, he recalled.

. . .

This exalted but fragile version of Gabrielle in his head did not allow him to love her with the unbridled passion he was capable of and to satisfy his needs, nor enable her to be herself. Fully.

"Would he have reacted in the same way to the letter had he not thought of her that way?" the thought mulling in his head repeatedly.

"Probably not", he concluded. His expectations of her and himself were perhaps romantic of a bygone era.

He loved her for what he could see she was underneath her protective shield, and he wanted to protect her.

He loved her for he could be when he was with her.

Deep down in his heart, he knew they both needed to become more 'human'.

Both were enamoured with the idealised version of self when they were together.

"You have shown me the best of me, the higher me I had lost", ... *drum drum* drumming in his head ...

. . .

… *"In your arms, I find safety like no other, and I can breathe deep, knowing you'll always keep me close and never hurt me"*.

"Safe", he thought, "she feels safe", he repeated.

He knew he always wanted her to feel secure, but not *just* so. He desired to satisfy her deepest needs and wants. ALL of her needs. And his own.

He had lived a very driven, passionate visceral life in every area before, except love, and he wanted that. Needed it. And now he could no longer ignore that; he knew neither could she.

… *"You cleaned up the mess and healed my wounds, and now I'm beginning to be whole again"*, … *drum drum.*

Something was stopping her, though, and she was not ready to talk about it.

He had noticed that Gabrielle had been particularly caring with him and more demonstrative than usual. He did not know how to encourage her to let go and let him in, if only a little more.

Mr Wonderful folded back the note and put it in his wallet.

• • •

"Time", he said. "It will take time", he repeated to convince himself.

Gabrielle was content that things were back to normal. Mr Wonderful was as chivalrous as usual and had not asked any more questions about the infamous letter.

He looked genuinely surprised and pleased she wrote to him and expressed her feelings.

"It wasn't as painful as I expected", she thought. "I should do it more often", she professed.

But life took over, and she forgot her pledge. Time passed by.

Mr Wonderful, however, wanted to know more, increasingly so. He realised that if he didn't push and prod, she wouldn't volunteer more insights into her past life or soul, for that matter.

"How long was the relationship?" he asked one day.

He knew it had ended but wished to learn more.

"It must have been significant, or she wouldn't have kept that letter".

. . .

"Why has it been so painful?" he couldn't figure it out.

"Why was she holding on and not abandoning herself to sheer pleasure when they were making love?"

One afternoon he had walked in on her as she was pleasuring herself. He stood there and watched silently, unknown to her. He witnessed her sheer abandonment of the flesh and joy in the act. Her face transfixed, her voice raucous.

He watched her touching herself aptly, knowing how to take it slowly or come quickly several times. But not with him. He was beginning to think it WAS him.

Gabrielle always seemed to squirm uncomfortably under his questions, glossing over her answer and changing subject swiftly.

Mr Wonderful knew he wanted more now. She was capable of more.

He tried to emulate what he had seen her doing.

He touched how she touched herself. He touched her where she touched herself.

. . .

But Gabrielle always managed to hold back to the point that he was sure she was faking orgasm 'to get it over with'.

"He deserved more", he thought.

And it wasn't just about sex, although he felt the need for a more visceral experience. It was about intimacy, the ability and willingness to be vulnerable with each other. And trust.

He had told her about his family, his abusive and philandering father who abandoned his mother and four other brothers, their struggle for a long time and how he made his fortune.

She knew his whole life story. He had been delicate about the details of his past relationships, although most of them had been played out in the press and were common knowledge, at least the gossip. Nevertheless, he had not kept anything from her and had answered any questions she asked.

Sometimes she seemed curious, and he was pleased she was showing an interest. But was not willing or able to do so herself.

Mr Wonderful had lived with Gabrielle in her Islington townhouse and realised she had never even spent the night at his.

. . .

He had given her a set of keys and made space in his wardrobe for her. Although he didn't necessarily want to move back or live in Belgravia, he wished she at least tried.

He hoped she did.
    He wanted her to.
    He waited for her to.

Time went by.

Gabrielle returned home from doing some errands to find a set of luggage by the front door. She didn't recognise them.

"Perhaps Mr Wonderful had planned a surprise getaway together?" she thought excitedly.

"Darling?" she called. She looked around and found him upstairs, sitting at her desk with his coat on.

"Hi", she said.

When he looked up, she realised something was wrong.

Mr Wonderful never thought he would ever come to this, saying goodbye.

．　．　．

Gabrielle was staring at him, looking fearful.

"My darling," he said. "I think it would be better if we take a break for a while."

Gabrielle looked at him incredulously; she could not believe he was saying that. Tears started falling down her cheeks.

"We can't ...."

"Why can't we be together?" she interrupted, weeping.

She was desperate to know why he had to say goodbye. "Surely not; I have misheard him".

She was desperate for him to answer why they couldn't be together.
    They loved each other, didn't they?

"I will always love you", he continued.

He got closer to her and then held her face in his hands while looking into those big brown eyes he fell in love with. He slowly patted her tears dry, trying to be strong for both of them. But it was hard, more difficult than he had imagined, and he couldn't control himself.

· · ·

He held her a bit longer and told her he would wait for her.

"My darling, your wounds are still open, and you are the only one who can truly heal them and make yourself whole. Be comfortable with every part of you and what you need and want".

Gabrielle couldn't grasp what he was saying.

"You shouldn't be scared of yourself and what you can be. But my darling, please do know that no matter how long it will take, if you still want me, Io ti aspetto".

She was confused. Soon he told her he would be able to hold her tight and never have to let go again, she heard.

Soon.

But the pain of saying goodbye was too much right now.

"Don't cry," he uttered with tears in his eyes.

'How long am I going to be without you?" she whispered to him.
    "How long?" she said, sobbing. "Please tell me".

•   •   •

"Don't forget me", he added, unsure how to answer.

"How could I ever?" she thought.

"I could never live my life fully without you," she said, unable to hold back her emotions, "You are the best part of me", and more tears started pouring down her cheeks.

"Let's make a date", he then declared. He was too scared, leaving it open-ended. He needed a date to look forward to.

"Let's meet on top of the Empire State Building", he proposed hopeful. They had watched *An Affair to Remember* many times together, and both loved how sweepingly romantic it was.

Gabrielle smiled through her tears, nodding.

"Six months from today", he was aching, thinking how he could live without her for so long. He knew though she needed the time.

"I will wait for you" he brought her closer to him as he wrapped his arms around her, time slipping out of his grip.

"I love you".

· · ·

Mr Wonderful hugged her tighter. Hoping that if he held on tighter to her, he wouldn't have to leave her.

Then he kissed her gently on the forehead, and, just like that, he was gone—every sign of him. The driver had picked up his luggage.

Gabrielle sat in silence for hours. Deep, profound emptiness inside of her.

The next day she received a plane ticket to New York dated precisely six months.

"Io ti aspetto", the accompanying note said.

Tears started streaming down her face when she thought she had no more to spare. In the following weeks, Paola and Martin rallied around her and tried their best to keep her company.

But, slowly, she found herself alone, starting again.

A long time passed before she could fully comprehend why he was gone.

· · ·

"I love you ",…. she murmured into the hot embrace they were sharing, but soon she felt her hands hold on to nothingness.

She woke up and opened her eyes slowly, scared to come to a reality where he was gone.

But once she did, Gabrielle realised she was alone once again. She wrapped her arms around herself. Holding herself, trying to feel his warmth again.

"I love you!" She shouted into the empty space, hoping wherever he was, he heard her.

Days and months went by.

Gabrielle's nightmares gradually subsided, replaced by vivid, joyful memories. Slowly but surely, she had begun to find her way back to herself. And she owed that to him.

She could see now.

Gabrielle had found her inner Isadora Duncan once again and learned to channel her desire and lust for life positively for her greater good. Not just in her new creative career this time.

· · ·

Instead of comparing now to the future or the past, she lived entirely in the present, savouring every moment.

With the death of her old self that she'd long been expecting and the birth of another, happier, higher one, Gabrielle stood erect and strong, drawing high and higher, until her stretched-out wings broke into fire.

She finally found a place to stand still, in love.

Find the love you seek by first finding the love within yourself. Learnt to rest in that place that is your true home

Sri Sri Ravi Shankar

DISCLAIMER

The Greatest Love of All is a work of fiction.

Although its form is that of a semi-autobiography (Gabrielle's) it is not one.

With the exception of public places, any resemblance to persons living or dead is coincidental. Space and time have been rearranged to suit the convenience of the book, memory has its own story to tell.

The opinions expressed are those of the characters and should not be confused with the author's.

AUTHOR'S NOTE

Thank you so much for reading *The Greatest Love*.

I hope you enjoyed this novella as an escapist story, or perhaps you also glimpsed something beneath as you read. A review would be much appreciated as it helps other readers discover the story.

Thanks so much.

If you sign up for my newsletter you'll be notified of giveaways, new releases and receive personal updates from behind the scenes of my business and books.

Go to www.thepeoplealchemist.com to get started.

Places in the book

I have set the story in real places in London and my beloved Islington. You can see some of the places here:

- Belgravia
- Canonbury Square and Gardens
- Empire State Building

Bibliography

I read books as part of my research amongst other things. Some of them together with other references include:

A Theory of Human Motivation - **Abraham Maslow**
Psycho-Cybernetics - **Maxwell Maltz**
Self Mastery Through Conscious Autosuggestion - **Émile Coué**
The Artist Way - **Julia Cameron**.
The Complete Reader - **Neville Goddard**, compiled and edited by **David Allen**
Tools of Titans - **Tim Ferris**

An Affair to Remember is a 1957 American romance film directed by Leo McCarey and starring Cary Grant and Deborah Kerr. It the story of two people in love who agree to reunite at the top of the Empire State Building in six months' time if they succeeded in ending their current relationships and starting new careers.
On the day of their rendezvous however, whilst hurrying to reach the place of the encounter, the woman is struck down by a car while crossing a street and is gravely injured.
Meanwhile, he is waiting for her unaware of the accident.
After many hours waiting, he leaves believing that she has rejected him. They reunite, of course, at the end of the movie.

Printed in Great Britain
by Amazon

85881479R00025